CUPID FROM BEAR CREEK
(THE PEACEFUL PILGRIM)

BY

ROBERT E. HOWARD

British Library Cataloguing-in-Publication Data
A catalogue record for this book is available from the
British Library

Robert E. Howard

Robert Ervin Howard was born in Peaster, Texas in 1906. During his youth, his family moved between a variety of Texan boomtowns, and Howard – a bookish and somewhat introverted child – was steeped in the violent myths and legends of the Old South. Although he loved reading and learning, Howard developed a distinctly Texan, hardboiled outlook on the world. He became a passionate fan of boxing, taking it up at an amateur level, and from the age of nine began to write adventure tales of semi-historical bloodshed. In 1919, when Howard was thirteen, his family moved to the Central Texas hamlet of Cross Plains, where he would stay for the rest of his life.

At fifteen Howard began to read the pulp magazines of the day, and to write more seriously. The December 1922 issue of his high school newspaper featured two of his stories, 'Golden Hope Christmas' and 'West is West'. In 1924 he sold his first piece – a short caveman tale titled 'Spear and Fang' – for $16 to the not-yet-famous *Weird Tales* magazine. He published with the magazine regularly over the next few years. 1929 was a breakout year for Howard, in that the 23-year-old writer began to sell to other magazines, such as *Ghost Stories* and *Argosy*, both of whom had previously sent him hundreds of rejection slips. In 1930, he began a correspondence with weird fiction master H. P. Lovecraft which ran up to his death six years later, and is regarded as one of the great correspondence cycles in all of fantasy literature.

It was partly due to Lovecraft's encouragement that Howard created his most famous character, Conan the Cimmerian. Conan – a barbarian-turned-King during the Hyborian Age, a mythical period of some 12,000 years ago – featured in seventeen *Weird Tales* stories between 1933 and 1936, and is now regarded as having spawned the 'sword and sorcery' genre, making Howard's influence on fantasy literature comparable to that of J. R. R. Tolkien's. The Conan stories have since been adapted many times, most famously in the series of films starring Arnold Schwarzenegger.

Howard was enjoying an all-time high in sales by the beginning of 1936, but he was also deeply upset by the ill health of his mother, who had fallen into a coma. On the morning of June 11, 1936, he asked an attending nurse whether she would ever recover, and the nurse replied negatively. Howard walked to his car, parked outside the family home in Cross Plains, and shot himself. He died eight hours later, aged just thirty.

Some day, maybe, when I'm a old man, I'll have sense enough to stay away from these new mining camps which springs up overnight like mushroomers. There was that time in Teton Gulch, for instance. It was a ill-advised moment when I stopped there on my way back to the Humbolts from the Yavapai country. I was a sheep for the shearing and I was shore plenty. And if some of the shearers got fatally hurt in the process, they needn't to blame me. I was acting in self-defense all the way through.

At first I aimed to pass right through Teton Gulch without stopping. I was in a hurry to git back to my home-country and find out was any misguided idjits trying to court Dolly Rixby, the belle of War Paint, in my absence. I hadn't heard from her since I left Bear Creek, five weeks before, which warn't surprizing, seeing as how she couldn't write, nor none of her family, and I couldn't of read it if they had. But they was a lot of young bucks around War Paint which could be counted on to start shining around her the minute my back was turnt.

But my thirst got the best of me, and I stopped in the camp. I was drinking me a dram at the bar of the Yaller Dawg Saloon and Hotel, when the bar-keep says, after studying me a spell, he says: "You must be Breckinridge Elkins, of Bear Creek."

I give the matter due consideration, and 'lowed as how I was.

"How come you knowed me?" I inquired suspiciously, because I hadn't never been in Teton Gulch before, and he says: "Well, I've heard tell of Breckinridge Elkins, and when I seen you, I figgered you must be him, because I don't see how they can be two men in the world that big. By the way, there's a friend of yore'n upstairs--Blink Wiltshaw, from War Paint. I've heered him brag about knowin' you personal. He's upstairs now, fourth door from the stair-head, on the left."

Now that there news interested me, because Blink was the most persistent of all them young mavericks which was trying to spark Dolly Rixby. Just the night before I left for Yavapai, I catched him coming out of her house, and was fixing to sweep the street with him when Dolly come out and stopped me and made us shake hands.

It suited me fine for him to be in Teton Gulch, or anywheres just so he warn't no-wheres nigh Dolly Rixby, so I thought I'd pass the time of day with him.

I went upstairs and knocked on the door, and bam! went a gun inside and a .45 slug ripped through the door and taken a nick out of my off-ear. Getting shot in the ear always did irritate me, so without waiting for no more exhibitions of hospitality, I give voice to my displeasure in a deafening beller and knocked the door off its hinges and busted into the room over its ruins.

For a second I didn't see nobody, but then I heard a kind of gurgle going on, and happened to remember that the door seemed kind of squishy underfoot when I tromped over it, so I knowed that whoever was in the room had got pinned under the door when I knocked it down.

So I reached under it and got him by the collar and hauled him out, and shore enough it was Blink Wiltshaw. He was limp as a lariat, and glassy-eyed and pale, and was still kind of trying to shoot me with his six-shooter when I taken it away from him.

"What the hell's the matter with you?" I demanded sternly, dangling him by the collar with one hand, whilst shaking him till his teeth rattled. "Didn't Dolly make us shake hands? What you mean by tryin' to 'sasserinate me through a hotel door?"

"Lemme down, Breck," he gasped. "I didn't know it was you. I thought it was Rattlesnake Harrison comin' after my gold."

SO I SOT HIM DOWN. HE grabbed a jug of licker and taken a swig, and his hand shook so he spilled half of it down his neck.

"Well?" I demanded. "Ain't you goin' to offer me a snort, dern it?"

"Excuse me, Breckinridge," he apolergized. "I'm so derned jumpy I dunno what I'm doin'. You see them buckskin pokes?" says he, p'inting at some bags on the bed.

5

"Them is plumb full of nuggets. I been minin' up the Gulch, and I hit a regular bonanza the first week. But it ain't doin' me no good."

"What you mean?" I demanded.

"These mountains is full of outlaws," says he. "They robs, and murders every man which makes a strike. The stagecoach has been stuck up so often nobody sends their dust out on it no more. When a man makes a pile he sneaks out through the mountains at night, with his gold on pack-mules. I aimed to do that last night. But them outlaws has got spies all over the camp, and I know they got me spotted. Rattlesnake Harrison's their chief, and he's a ring-tailed he-devil. I been squattin' over this here gold with my pistol in fear and tremblin', expectin' 'em to come right into camp after me. I'm dern nigh loco!"

And he shivered and cussed kind of whimpery, and taken another dram, and cocked his pistol and sot there shaking like he'd saw a ghost or two.

"You got to help me, Breckinridge," he said desperately. "You take this here gold out for me, willya? The outlaws don't know you. You could hit the old Injun path south of the camp and foller it to Hell-Wind Pass. The Chawed-Ear--Wahpeton stage goes through there about sun-down. You could put the gold on the stage there, and they'd take it on to Wahpeton. Harrison wouldn't never think of holdin' it up after it left Hell-Wind. They always holds it up this side of the Pass."

"What I want to risk my neck for you for?" I demanded bitterly, memories of Dolly Rixby rising up before me. "If you ain't got the guts to tote out yore own gold--"

"T'ain't altogether the gold, Breck," says he. "I'm tryin' to git married, and--"

"Married?" says I. "Here? In Teton Gulch? To a gal in Teton Gulch?"

"Married to a gal in Teton Gulch," he avowed. "I was aimin' to git hitched tomorrer, but they ain't a preacher or justice of the peace in camp to tie the knot. But her uncle the Reverant Rembrandt Brockton is a circuit rider, and he's due to pass through Hell-Wind on his way to Wahpeton today. I was aimin' to sneak out last night, hide in the hills till the stage come through, then put the gold on the stage and bring Brother Rembrandt back with me. But yesterday I learnt Harrison's spies was watchin' me, and I'm scairt to go. Now Brother Rembrandt will go on to Wahpeton, not knowin' he's needed here, and no tellin' when I'll be able to git married--"

"Hold on," I said hurried, doing some quick thinking. I didn't want this here wedding to fall through. The more Blink was married to some gal in Teton, the less he could marry Dolly Rixby.

"Blink," I said, grasping his hand warmly, "let it never be said that a Elkins ever turned down a friend in distress. I'll take yore gold to Hell-Wind Pass and bring back Brother Rembrandt."

Blink fell onto my neck and wept with joy. "I'll never forget this, Breckinridge," says he, "and I bet you won't neither! My hoss and pack-mule are in the stables behind the saloon."

"I don't need no pack-mule," I says. "Cap'n Kidd can pack the dust easy."

CAP'N KIDD WAS GETTING fed out in the corral next to the hotel. I went out there and got my saddle-bags, which is a lot bigger'n most saddle-bags, because all my plunder has to be made to fit my size. They're made outa three-ply elkskin, stitched with rawhide thongs, and a wildcat couldn't claw his way out of 'em.

I noticed quite a bunch of men standing around the corral looking at Cap'n Kidd, but thought nothing of it, because he is a hoss which naturally attracts attention. But whilst I was getting my saddle-bags, a long lanky cuss with long yaller whiskers come up and said, says he: "Is that yore hoss in the corral?"

If he ain't he ain't nobody's," I says.

"Well, he looks a whole lot like a hoss that was stole off my ranch six months ago," he said, and I seen ten or fifteen hard-looking hombres gathering around me. I laid down my saddle-bags sudden-like and reached for my guns, when it occurred to me that if I had a fight there I might git arrested and it would interfere with me bringing Brother Rembrandt in for the wedding.

"If that there is yore hoss," I said, "you ought to be able to lead him out of that there corral."

"Shore I can," he says with a oath. "And what's more, I aim'ta."

He looked at me suspiciously, but he taken up a rope and clumb the fence and started toward Cap'n Kidd which was chawing on a block of hay in the middle of the corral. Cap'n Kidd throwed up his head and laid back his ears and showed his teeth, and Jake stopped sudden and turned pale.

"I--I don't believe that there is my hoss, after all!" says he.

"Put that lasso on him!" I roared, pulling my right-hand gun. "You say he's yore'n; I say he's mine. One of us is a liar and a hoss-thief, and I aim to prove which. Gwan, before I festoons yore system with lead polka-dots!"

He looked at me and he looked at Cap'n Kidd, and he turned bright green all over. He looked agen at my .45 which I now had cocked and p'inted at his long neck, which his adam's apple was going up and down like a monkey on a pole, and he begun to aidge toward Cap'n Kidd again, holding the rope behind him and sticking out one hand.

"Whoa, boy," he says kind of shudderingly. "Whoa--good old feller--nice hossie--whoa, boy--ow!"

He let out a awful howl as Cap'n Kidd made a snap and bit a chunk out of his hide. He turned to run but Cap'n Kidd wheeled and let fly both heels which caught Jake in the seat of the britches, and his shriek of despair was horrible to hear as he went head-first through the corral fence into a hoss-trough on the other side. From this he ariz dripping water, blood and profanity, and he shook a quivering fist at me and croaked: "You derned murderer! I'll have yore life for this!"

"I don't hold no conversation with hoss-thieves," I snorted, and picked up my saddle-bags and stalked through the crowd which give back in a hurry.

I TAKEN THE SADDLE-BAGS up to Blink's room, and told him about Jake, thinking he'd be amoosed, but got a case of aggers again, and said: "That was one of Harrison's men! He meant to take yore hoss. It's a old trick, and honest folks don't dare interfere. Now they got you spotted! What'll you do?"

"Time, tide and a Elkins waits for no man!" I snorted, dumping the gold into the saddle-bags. "If that yaller-whiskered coyote wants any trouble, he can git a bellyfull. Don't worry, yore gold will be safe in my saddle-bags. It's as good as in the Wahpeton stage right now. And by midnight

I'll be back with Brother Rembrandt Brockton to hitch you up with his niece."

"Don't yell so loud," begged Blink. "The cussed camp's full of spies. Some of 'em may be downstairs now, listenin'."

"I warn't speakin' above a whisper," I said indignantly.

"That bull's beller may pass for a whisper on Bear Creek," says he, wiping off the sweat, "but I bet they can hear it from one end of the Gulch to the other, at least."

It's a pitable sight to see a man with a case of the scairts; I shook hands with him and left him pouring red licker down his gullet like it was water, and I swung the saddle-bags over my shoulder and went downstairs, and the bar-keep leaned over the bar and whispered to me: "Look out for Jake Roman! He was in here a minute ago, lookin' for trouble. He pulled out just before you come down, but he won't be forgittin' what yore hoss done to him!"

"Not when he tries to set down, he won't," I agreed, and went on out to the corral, and they was a crowd of men watching Cap'n Kidd eat his hay, and one of 'em seen me and hollered: "Hey, boys, here comes the giant! He's goin' to saddle that man-eatin' monster! Hey, Bill! Tell the boys at the bar!"

And here come a whole passel of fellers running out of all the saloons, and they lined the corral fence solid, and started laying bets whether I'd git the saddle on Cap'n Kidd or git my brains kicked out. I thought miners must all be crazy. They ought've knowed I was able to saddle my own hoss.

Well, I saddled him and throwed on the saddle-bags and clumb aboard, and he pitched about ten jumps like he always does when I first fork him--t'warn't nothing, but them miners hollered like wild Injuns. And when he accidentally bucked hisself and me through the fence and knocked down a section of it along with fifteen men which was setting on the top-rail, the way they howled you'd of thought something terrible had happened. Me and Cap'n Kidd don't generally bother about gates. We usually makes our own through whatever happens to be in front of us. But them miners is a weakly breed, because as I rode out of town I seen the crowd dipping four or five of 'em into a hoss-trough to bring 'em to, on account of Cap'n Kidd having accidentally tromped on 'em.

WELL, I RODE OUT OF THE Gulch and up the ravine to the south, and come out into the high timbered country, and hit the old Injun trail Blink had told me about. It warn't traveled much. I didn't meet nobody after I left the Gulch. I figgered to hit Hell-Wind Pass at least a hour before sun-down which would give me plenty of time. Blink said the stage passed through there about sun-down. I'd have to bring back Brother Rembrandt on Cap'n Kidd, I reckoned, but that there hoss can carry double and still out-run and out-last any other hoss in the State of Nevada. I figgered on getting back to Teton about midnight or maybe a little later.

After I'd went several miles I come to Apache Canyon, which was a deep, narrer gorge, with a river at the bottom which went roaring and foaming along betwixt rock walls a hundred and fifty feet high. The old trail hit the rim at a place where the canyon warn't only about seventy foot wide, and somebody had felled a whopping big pine tree on one side so it fell acrost and made a foot-bridge, where a man could walk acrost. They'd once been a gold strike in Apache Canyon, and a big camp there, but now it was plumb abandoned and nobody lived anywheres near it.

I turned east and follered the rim for about half a mile. Here I come into a old wagon road which was just about growed up with saplings now, but it run down into a ravine into the bed of the canyon, and they was a bridge acrost the river which had been built during the days of the gold rush. Most of it had done been washed away by head-rises, but a man could still ride a horse across what was left. So I done so and rode up a ravine on the other side, and come out on high ground again.

I'd rode a few hundred yards past the ravine when somebody said: "Hey!" and I wheeled with both guns in my hands. Out of the bresh s'antered a tall gent in a long frock tail coat and broad-brimmed hat.

"Who air you and what the hell you mean by hollerin' 'Hey!' at me?" I demanded courteously, p'inting my guns at him. A Elkins is always perlite.

"I am the Reverant Rembrandt Brockton, my good man," says he. "I am on my way to Teton Gulch to unite my niece and a young man of that camp in the bonds of holy matrimony."

"The he--you don't say!" I says. "Afoot?"

"I alit from the stage-coach at--ah--Hades-Wind Pass," says he. "Some very agreeable cowboys happened to be awaiting the stage there, and they offered to escort me to Teton."

"How come you knowed yore niece was wantin' to be united in acrimony?" I ast.

"The cowboys informed me that such was the case," says he.

"Where-at are they now?" I next inquore.

"The mount with which they supplied me went lame a little while ago," says he. "They left me here while they went to procure another from a near-by ranch-house."

"I dunno who'd have a ranch anywheres near here," I muttered. "They ain't got much sense leavin' you here by yore high lonesome."

"You mean to imply there is danger?" says he, blinking mildly at me.

"These here mountains is lousy with outlaws which would as soon kyarve a preacher's gullet as anybody's," I said, and then I thought of something else. "Hey!" I says. "I thought the stage didn't come through the Pass till sundown?"

"Such was the case," says he. "But the schedule has been altered."

"Heck!" I says. "I was aimin' to put this here gold on it which my saddle-bags is full of. Now I'll have to take it back to Teton with me. Well, I'll bring it out tomorrer and catch the stage then. Brother Rembrandt, I'm Breckinridge Elkins, of Bear Creek, and I come out here to meet you and escort you back to the Gulch, so's you could unite yore niece and Blink Wiltshaw in the holy bounds of alimony. Come on. We'll ride double."

"But I must await my cowboy friends!" he said. "Ah, here they come now!"

I looked over to the east and seen about fifteen men ride into sight out of the bresh and move toward us. One was leading a hoss without no saddle onto it.

"Ah, my good friends!" beamed Brother Rembrandt. "They have procured a mount for me, even as they promised."

He hauled a saddle out of the bresh, and says: "Would you please saddle my horse for me when they get here? I should be delighted to hold your rifle while you did so."

I started to hand him my Winchester, when the snap of a twig under a hoss's hoof made me whirl quick. A feller had just rode out of a thicket about a hundred yards south of me, and he was raising a Winchester to his shoulder. I recognized him instantly. If us Bear Creek folks didn't have eyes like a hawk, we'd never live to git growed. It was Jake Roman!

Our Winchesters banged together. His lead fanned my ear and mine knocked him end-ways out of his saddle.

"Cowboys, hell!" I roared. "Them's Harrison's outlaws! I'll save you, Brother Rembrandt!"

I SWOOPED HIM UP WITH one arm and gouged Cap'n Kidd with the spurs and he went from there like a thunderbolt with its tail on fire. Them outlaws come on with wild yells. I ain't in the habit of running from people, but I was afeared they might do the Reverant harm if it come to a close fight, and if he stopped a hunk of lead, Blink might not git to marry his niece, and might git disgusted and go back to War Paint and start sparking Dolly Rixby again.

I was heading back for the canyon, aiming to make a stand in the ravine if I had to, and them outlaws was killing their hosses trying to git to the bend of the trail ahead of me, and cut me off. Cap'n Kidd was running with his belly to the ground, but I'll admit Brother Rembrandt warn't helping me much. He was laying across my saddle with his arms and laigs waving wildly because I hadn't had time to set him comfortable, and when the horn jobbed him in the belly he uttered some words I wouldn't of expected to hear spoke by a minister of the gospel.

Guns begun to crack and lead hummed past us, and Brother Rembrandt twisted his head around and screamed: "Stop that shootin', you--sons of--! You'll hit me!"

I thought it was kind of selfish of Brother Rembrandt not to mention me, too, but I said: "T'ain't no use to remonstrate with them skunks, Reverant. They ain't got no respeck for a preacher even."

But to my amazement the shooting stopped, though them bandits yelled louder'n ever and flogged their cayuses. But about that time I seen they had me cut off from the lower canyon crossing, so I wrenched Cap'n Kidd into the old Injun trace and headed straight for the canyon rim as hard as he could hammer, with the bresh lashing and snapping around us and slapping Brother Rembrandt in the face when it whipped back. The outlaws yelled and wheeled in behind us, but Cap'n Kidd drawed away from them with every stride, and the canyon rim loomed just ahead of us.

"Pull up, you jack-eared son of Baliol!" howled Brother Rembrandt. "You'll go over the edge!"

"Be at ease, Reverant," I reassured him. "We're goin' over the log."

"Lord have mercy on my soul!" he squalled, and shet his eyes and grabbed a stirrup leather with both hands, and then Cap'n Kidd went over that log like thunder rolling on Jedgment Day.

I doubt if they is another hoss west of the Pecos which would bolt out onto a log foot-bridge acrost a canyon a hundred fifty foot deep like that, but they ain't nothing in this world Cap'n Kidd's scairt of except maybe me. He didn't slacken his speed none. He streaked acrost that log like it was a quarter-track, with the bark and splinters flying from under his hoofs, and if one foot had slipped a inch, it would of been Sally bar the door. But he didn't slip, and we was over and on the other side almost before you could catch yore breath.

"You can open yore eyes now, Brother Rembrandt," I said kindly, but he didn't say nothing. He'd fainted. I shook him to wake him up, and in a flash he come to and give a shriek and grabbed my laig like a b'ar trap. I reckon he thought we was still on the log. I was trying to pry him loose when Cap'n Kidd chose that moment to run under a low-hanging oak tree limb. That's his idee of a joke. That there hoss has got a great sense of humor.

I looked up just in time to see the limb coming, but not in time to dodge it. It was as big around as my thigh, and it took me smack acrost the wish-bone. We was going full speed, and something had to give way. It was the girths--both of 'em. Cap'n Kidd went out from under me, and me and Brother Rembrandt and the saddle hit the ground together.

I JUMPED UP BUT BROTHER Rembrandt laid there going: "Wug wug wug!" like water running out of a busted jug. And then I seen them outlaws had dismounted off of their hosses and was corning acrost the bridge single file, with their Winchesters in their hands.

I didn't waste no time shooting them misguided idjits. I run to the end of the foot-bridge, ignoring the slugs they slung at me. It was purty pore shooting, because they warn't shore of their footing, and didn't aim good. So I only got one bullet in the hind laig and was creased three or four other unimportant places--not enough to bother about.

I bent my knees and got hold of the end of the tree and heaved up with it, and them outlaws hollered and fell along it like ten pins, and dropped their Winchesters and grabbed holt of the log. I given it a shake and shook some of 'em off like persimmons off a limb after a frost, and then I swung the butt around clear of the rim and let go, and it went down end over end into the river a hundred and fifty feet below, with a dozen men still hanging onto it and yelling blue murder.

A regular geyser of water splashed up when they hit, and the last I seen of 'em they was all swirling down the river together in a thrashing tangle of arms and laigs and heads.

I remember Brother Rembrandt and run back to where he'd fell, but was already onto his feet. He was kind of pale and wild-eyed and his laigs kept bending under him, but he had hold of the saddle-bags and was trying to drag 'em into a thicket, mumbling kind of dizzily to hisself.

"It's all right now, Brother Rembrandt," I said kindly. "Them outlaws is plumb horse-de-combat now, as the French say. Blink's gold is safe."

"--!" says Brother Rembrandt, pulling two guns from under his coat tails, and if I hadn't grabbed him, he would of undoubtedly shot me. We rassled around and I protested: "Hold on, Brother Rembrandt! I ain't no outlaw. I'm yore friend, Breckinridge Elkins. Don't you remember?"

His only reply was a promise to eat my heart without no seasoning, and he then sunk his teeth into my ear and started to chaw it off, whilst gouging for my eyes with both thumbs and spurring me severely in the hind laigs. I seen he was out of his head from fright and the fall he got, so I said sorrerfully: "Brother Rembrandt, I hate to do this. It hurts me more'n it does you, but we cain't waste time like this. Blink is waitin' to git married." And with a sigh I busted him over the head with the butt of my six-shooter, and he fell over and twitched a few times and then lay limp.

"Pore Brother Rembrandt," I sighed sadly. "All I hope is I ain't addled yore brains so you've forgot the weddin' ceremony."

So as not to have no more trouble with him when, and if, he come to, I tied his arms and laigs with pieces of my lariat, and taken his weppins which was most surprizing arms for a circuit rider. His pistols had the triggers out of 'em, and they was three notches on the butt of one, and four on the other'n. Moreover he had a bowie knife in his boot, and a deck of marked kyards and a pair of loaded dice in his hip-pocket. But that warn't none of my business.

About the time I finished tying him up, Cap'n Kidd come back to see if he'd killed me or just crippled me for life. To show him I can take a joke too, I give him a kick in the belly, and when he could git his breath again, and undouble hisself, I throwed the saddle on him. I spliced the girths with the rest of my lariat, and put Brother Rembrandt in the saddle and clumb on behind and we headed for Teton Gulch.

After a hour or so Brother Rembrandt come to and says kind of dizzily: "Was anybody saved from the typhoon?"

"Yo're all right, Brother Rembrandt," I assured him. "I'm takin' you to Teton Gulch."

"I remember," he muttered. "It all comes back to me. Damn Jake Roman! I thought it was a good idea, but it seems I was mistaken. I thought we had an ordinary human being to deal with. I know when I'm licked. I'll give you a thousand dollars to let me go."

"Take it easy, Brother Rembrandt," I soothed, seeing he was still delirious. "We'll be to Teton in no time."

"I don't want to go to Teton!" he hollered.

"You got to," I said. "You got to unite yore niece and Blink Wiltshaw in the holy bums of parsimony."

"To hell with Blink Wiltshaw and my--niece!" he yelled.

"You ought to be ashamed usin' sech langwidge, and you a minister of the gospel," I reproved him sternly. His reply would of curled a Piute's hair.

I was so scandalized I made no reply. I was just fixing to untie him, so's he could ride more comfortable, but I thought if he was that crazy, I better not. So I give no heed to his ravings which growed more and more unbearable. In all my born days I never seen such a preacher.

IT WAS SHORE A RELIEF to me to sight Teton at last. It was night when we rode down the ravine into the Gulch, and the dance halls and saloons was going full blast. I rode up behind the Yaller Dawg Saloon and hauled Brother Rembrandt off with me and sot him on his feet, and he said, kind of despairingly: "For the last time, listen to reason. I got fifty thousand dollars cached up in the hills. I'll give you every cent if you'll untie me."

"I don't want no money," I said. "All I want is for you to marry yore niece and Blink Wiltshaw. I'll untie you then."

"All right," he said. "All right! But untie me now!"

I was just fixing to do it, when the bar-keep come out with a lantern and he shone it on our faces and said in a startled tone: "Who the hell is that with you, Elkins?"

"You wouldn't never suspect it from his langwidge," I says, "but it's the Reverant Rembrandt Brockton."

"Are you crazy?" says the bar-keep. "That's Rattlesnake Harrison!"

"I give up," said my prisoner. "I'm Harrison. I'm licked. Lock me up somewhere away from this lunatic."

I was standing in a kind of daze, with my mouth open, but now I woke up and bellered: "What? Yo're Harrison? I see it all now! Jake Roman overheard me talkin' to Blink Wiltshaw, and rode off and fixed it with you to fool me like you done, so's to git Blink's gold! That's why you wanted to hold my Winchester whilst I saddled yore cayuse."

"How'd you ever guess it?" he sneered. "We ought to have shot you from ambush like I wanted to, but Jake wanted to catch you alive and torture you to death account of your horse bitin' him. The fool must have lost his head at the last minute and decided to shoot you after all. If you hadn't recognized him we'd had you surrounded and stuck up before you knew what was happening."

"But now the real preacher's gone on to Wahpeton!" I hollered. "I got to foller him and bring him back--"

"Why, he's here," said one of the men which was gathering around us. "He come in with his niece a hour ago on the stage from War Paint."

"War Paint?" I howled, hit in the belly by a premonition. I run into the saloon, where they was a lot of people, and there was Blink and a gal holding hands in front of a old man with a long white beard, and he had a book in his hand, and t'other'in lifted in the air. He was saying: "--And I now pronounces you-all man and wife. Them which God had j'ined together let no snake-hunter put asunder."

"Dolly!" I yelled. Both of 'em jumped about four foot and whirled, and Dolly Rixby jumped in front of Blink and spread her arms like she was shooing chickens.

"Don't you tech him, Breckinridge Elkins!" she hollered. "I just married him and I don't aim for no Humbolt grizzly to spile him!"

"But I don't sabe all this--" I said dizzily, nervously fumbling with my guns which is a habit of mine when upsot.

Everybody in the wedding party started ducking out of line, and Blink said hurriedly: "It's this way, Breck. When I made my pile so onexpectedly quick, I sent for Dolly to come and marry me like she'd promised the day after you left for the Yavapai. I was aimin' to take my gold out today, like I told you, so me and Dolly could go to San Francisco on our honeymoon, but I learnt Harrison's gang was watchin' me, just like I told you. I wanted to git my gold out, and I wanted to git you out of the way before Dolly and her uncle got here on the War Paint stage, so I told you that lie about Brother Rembrandt bein' on the Wahpeton stage. It was the only lie."

"You said you was marryin' a gal in Teton," I accused fiercely.

"Well," says he, "I did marry her in Teton. You know, Breck, all's fair in love and war."

"Now, now, boys," said Brother Rembrandt--the real one, I mean. "The gal's married, yore rivalry is over, and they's no use holdin' grudges. Shake hands and be friends."

"All right," I said heavily. No man cain't say I ain't a good loser. I was cut deep but I concealed my busted heart.

Leastways I concealed it all I was able to. Them folks which says I crippled Blink Wiltshaw with malice aforethought is liars which I'll sweep the road with when I catches 'em. When my emotions is wrought up I unconsciously uses more of my strength than I realizes. I didn't aim to break Blink's arm when I shook hands with him; it was just the stress of my emotions. Likewise it was Dolly's fault that her Uncle Rembrandt got throwed out a winder and some others got their heads banged. When she busted me with that cuspidor I knew that our love was dead forever. Tears come into my eyes as I waded through the crowd, and I had to move fast to keep from making a fool of myself. Them that was flang out of my way ought to have knowed it was done more in sorrer than in anger.

www.ingramcontent.com/pod-product-compliance
Lightning Source LLC
Chambersburg PA
CBHW030244180626
46810CB00008B/3278